THE AVION MY UNCLE FLEW

"Full of vitality and suspense . . . The most ingenious feature of the book is the fascinating way in which Johnny learned to speak French. This is a wholly new idea in a story, worthy of special notice." —*The Horn Book*

"It is one of the few instances when the most transitory form of fiction—the mystery-adventure-spy story—makes a permanent contribution not only to boys' books but to understanding how a boy's mind works and how, on occasion, he can change it." —*New York Herald Tribune*

Mon oncle threw le maire out of the door

[page 134]

The Avion My Uncle Flew

by Cyrus Fisher

Pictures by Richard Floethe

PUFFIN BOOKS

PUFFIN BOOKS
Published by the Penguin Group
Penguin Books USA Inc., 375 Hudson Street, New York, New York 10014, U.S.A.
Penguin Books Ltd, 27 Wrights Lane, London W8 5TZ, England
Penguin Books Australia Ltd, Ringwood, Victoria, Australia
Penguin Books Canada Ltd, 10 Alcorn Avenue, Toronto, Ontario, Canada M4V 3B2
Penguin Books (N.Z.) Ltd, 182–190 Wairau Road, Auckland 10, New Zealand

Penguin Books Ltd, Registered Offices: Harmondsworth, Middlesex, England

First published in the United States of America by Appleton-Century-Crofts,
an affiliate of Meredith Press, 1946
Published in Puffin Books, 1993

1 3 5 7 9 10 8 6 4 2

CIP data available from the Library of Congress
ISBN 0-14-036487-0
Printed in the United States of America